Finny
Fairy Fish

Written by Diana McCaulay

Illustrated by Stacey Byer

Collins

There once was a fish named Phineas,
Finny for short, who lived with Cadeem
the Congatoni on a coral reef in the warm
Caribbean Sea.

Now Finny had never seen himself, so he
thought he was a pinky-orange Congatoni
with bulgy eyes like all the others. But he was
a rare Fairy Fish, half purple
and half orange.

One day, Finny found a broken conch shell. He turned it over and saw himself. He was not pinky-orange with bulgy eyes! He was half PURPLE and half ORANGE.

He burst into fish tears and hid.

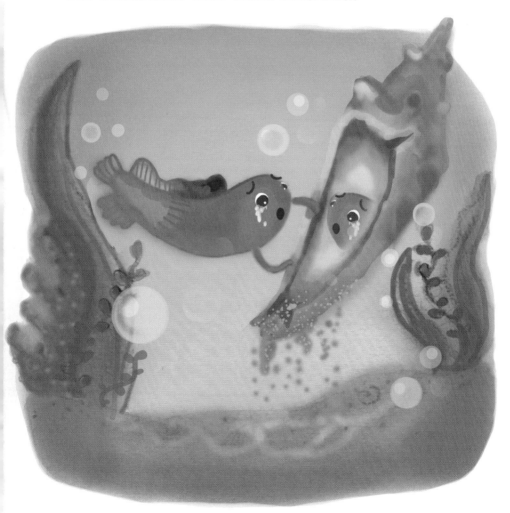

"Finny!" called Cadeem. "It's feeding time."

But Finny did not come out.

"Oh, Cadeem," he bubbled from his hiding place, "I saw myself in a conch shell and I'm very, very ugly!"

"You are *not* ugly, Finny! You are a beautiful Fairy Fish."

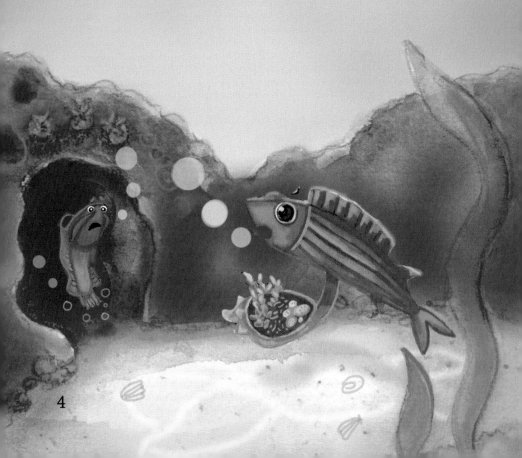

But Finny did not believe Cadeem. He refused to bubble, swim or play. He stopped eating and his colours started to fade.

"What shall we do?" Cadeem asked his best friend, Mara the Moray Eel.

Mara thought. "We have to find a wise elder. I know! Donette the Dolphin!"

"But she lives in the Deep Sea where a Congatoni cannot go!" objected Cadeem.

"You can find her, my old friend. I'll look after Finny while you're gone."

Cadeem stared into the Deep Sea and he was afraid.

Then a HUGE Blue Marlin swam up. Cadeem trembled but he did not hide.

"Why are you here, Congatoni?" gurgled the Blue Marlin.

"I need the advice of D-Donette the D-Dolphin," stammered Cadeem.

"Tell me your story," gurgled the Blue Marlin.

So Cadeem told the Blue Marlin
about Finny the Fairy Fish seeing
himself in the mirror for
the first time.

"You are brave and loving,
Congatoni. I'll help you find
Elder Donette.
Come."

The Blue Marlin and the Congatoni swam
and swam until Cadeem's strength was
almost spent.

"Elder Donette lives over there,"
said the Blue Marlin, stopping.
"Swim a loop-the-loop and
she might come to you."

"Might?" bubbled Cadeem.

"Might. I wish you well, brave Congatoni."
Then the Blue Marlin was gone.

Cadeem was very tired, but somehow he swam a loop-the-loop.

He waited, alone in all that blue.

Elder Donette swam up! "Speak, Congatoni!" she bubbled. "Why are you here in the Deep Sea?"

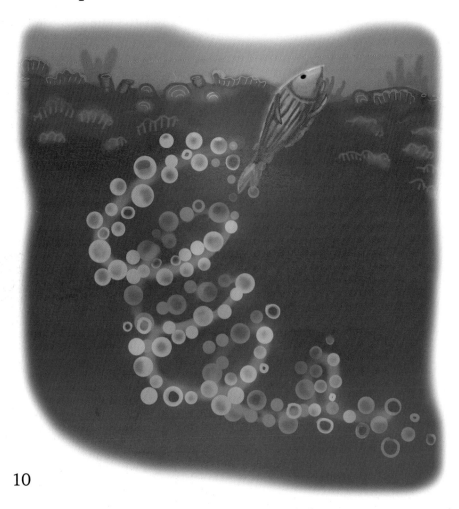

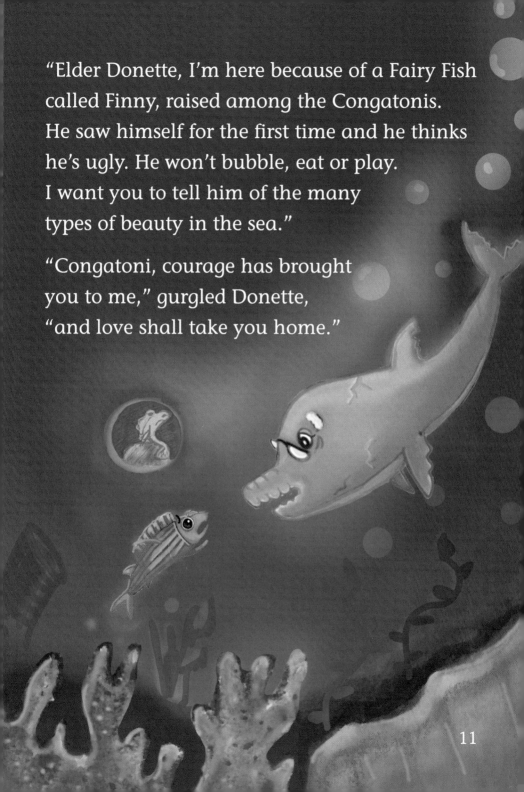

"Elder Donette, I'm here because of a Fairy Fish
called Finny, raised among the Congatonis.
He saw himself for the first time and he thinks
he's ugly. He won't bubble, eat or play.
I want you to tell him of the many
types of beauty in the sea."

"Congatoni, courage has brought
you to me," gurgled Donette,
"and love shall take you home."

Donette raced through the Deep Sea, creating a wave which carried Cadeem along, and soon they saw the coral reef ahead.

"Sandy Pool is over here, right?" gurgled Donette.

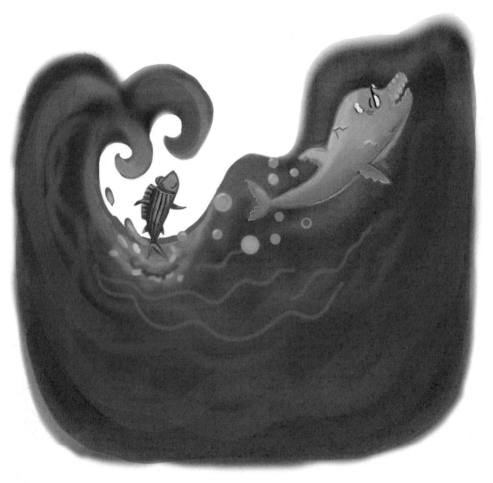

Before Cadeem could answer, the dolphin launched herself over the reef.

"Bring Finny to me," she bubbled to Cadeem.

"I will," said Cadeem.

Back at the Congatonis' rock, Mara was trying to get Finny to eat.

"Cadeem!" Mara yelled, when her old friend appeared. "Did you find Elder Donette? Finny is in a bad way."

"I did," said Cadeem. "She's here to see you, Finny."

"Me?" Finny grunted, and his eyes opened a little.

"Come with me," bubbled Cadeem.

Finny left his rock home with Cadeem
and Mara, and the other Congatonis followed.

"Greetings, Finny!" said Elder Donette.
"Why won't you bubble, eat or play?"

"El-el-der," wailed Finny, "because I'm not a Congatoni like all the others!"

"Now listen well, young Finny," said Elder Donette. "To be different is to be blessed. We don't want a sea where every fish is the same! The colour of your scales or shape of fin or tail don't matter. You were loved before you saw yourself. You are loved so much that a Congatoni would brave the Deep Sea to find me."

At these words, a great joy entered
Finny's heart. And he was suddenly hungry.

"Celebrate, Congatonis!"
gurgled Elder Donette.
"Cadeem the Courageous
has returned and now
you all know
what matters."

Then she launched
herself from
the Sandy Pool
and was gone.

The young Congatonis bubbled with
excitement and suggested a game of
Conga Polo.

"Th-hank you," Finny bubbled to Cadeem.

"You're not going to play Conga Polo?"
Cadeem asked.

"Lunch first," bubbled Finny.
"*Then*, Conga Polo!"

Finny swam a perfect loop-the-loop.
Already, his beautiful colours were back.

An emotional journey

sadness

tiredness

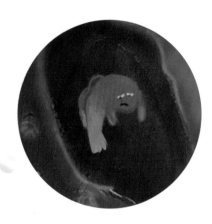

fear

determination

worry

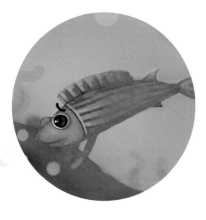

love

Ideas for reading

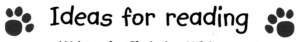

Written by Christine Whitney
Primary Literacy Consultant

Reading objectives:
- discuss the sequence of events in books
- make inferences on the basis of what is being said and done
- predict what might happen on the basis of what has been read so far

Spoken language objectives:
- ask relevant question; speculate, imagine and explore ideas through talk;
- participate in discussions

Curriculum links: Science – children should use the local environment throughout the year to explore and answer questions about animals in their habitat; Writing – write narratives about personal experiences and those of others, write for different purposes

Word count: 778

Interest words: coral reef, conch shell, scales, loop-the-loop

Resources: paper, pencils and crayons for writing and drawing

Build a context for reading

- Before children read the book, show them pictures of a Fairy Fish, a Congatoni (Squirrel Fish), a Blue Marlin, a Moray Eel and a dolphin. Ask them if they have ever seen these creatures and if they know anything about them.

- Read the blurb on the back cover of the book. Ask children to talk to each other about how Finny is different to his friends. What do they think is *truly important?*

Understand and apply reading strategies

- Read pp2–3. Ask children to retell what happened when Finny found a broken conch shell.

- Continue to read to p11. Ask children why Cadeem swam to the Deep Sea to speak to Elder Donette.